Oliver Brightside: You Don't Want That Penny

Christopher Manzo

Illustrated by Lisa Adams

All About Kids Publishing

A special thank you to Stephen Zmina

All About Kids Publishing
P.O. Box 159
Gilroy, CA 95021
www.allaboutkidspub.com
@allaboutkidspub

Library of Congress Cataloging-in-Publication Data

Names: Manzo, Christopher, author. | Adams, Lisa, 1951- illustrator.
Title: Oliver Brightside : you don't want that penny / by Christopher Manzo ;
illustrated by Lisa Adams.
Description: Gilroy : All About Kids Publishing, [2016] | Summary: Oliver
Brightside finds a heads up penny on a sidewalk and remembers it will
bring him good luck so he asks around his New York neighborhood what he
can buy with it, but after he is told of the penny's limited value his
good luck helps him find a way to spend it and make a new friend.

Identifiers: LCCN 2015045396 | ISBN 9780996375641 (hardcover picture book :
alk. paper)
Subjects: | CYAC: Money--Fiction. | Luck--Fiction. | Friendship--Fiction. |
New York (N.Y.)--Fiction.
Classification: LCC PZ7.1.M3695 Ol 2016 | DDC [E]--dc23

For Mom and Dad.
I love you both.

To Albie, Lauren, Jonathan Hadaya, my dear friends
at Sirens Media, and the wonderful team at
All About Kids Publishing — thank you for picking
up the penny that others ignored.

It's another boring day in New York City for Oliver Brightside, but he has no idea that his luck is about to change.

Whoa, look at that! A heads up penny!

He couldn't believe someone would leave something as great as a penny on the sidewalk.

"Find a penny, pick it up,
all day long you'll have good luck!"

An unfamiliar voice spoke to Oliver. "That's silly! I fly up in the sky every day, and see thousands of pennies, if they are such good luck, why do so many people drop them?"

Oliver never spoke to a pigeon before, and now he was happy that he hadn't.

"No, Mr. Pigeon, pennies are good luck, and I'm going to show you!"

9

Oliver set out to find a more familiar face, so he walked over to a big construction site and found the nearest worker.

"Excuse me sir, I just found this penny, do you have any idea what I can buy with it?"

The man looked at Oliver confused, "Ha! You can't do nuttin with a penny these days kid."

11

It wasn't the answer he wanted but he wasn't going to stop looking.

There are hot dog carts on every corner of the Big Apple, surely they will accept a shiny new penny, he thought to himself.

"What do you have for a penny?" Oliver asked at the hot dog stand.

"It costs a dime just for mustard! Dimes are smaller than pennies and worth more, what's that tell you? Nobody wants that penny!" said the hot dog vendor.

HOT DOGS

Oliver turned and let out a big sigh. He felt discouraged, but seeing the pigeon's smirk gave him renewed determination.

He walked to Columbus Circle and sat down.

"There has to be someone who could use a penny." Oliver said to himself aloud.

"Look at the man on that coin, he isn't even smiling."

Oliver looked up and couldn't believe his eyes. A talking statue?!

"I would smile if I were famous enough to be on a coin. Well, maybe not if I were only worth one measly cent." the statue declared.

I can see that I won't get any help here, Oliver thought.

Oliver had an idea…a cab driver! Surely he could get across town for a penny.

"*Fuhgeddaboudit*," the cabbie yelled, "it costs $5.00 to get across town, do you know how many pennies that would take? *Five hundred!*"

19

Oliver knew just who to talk to, the world famous Statue of Liberty. She'll know what to do with the penny. As he rode on the ferry he felt encouraged.

"Do you know what pennies are made of?"
Lady Liberty asked.

Oliver shrugged.

"Like me, pennies are made of copper.
I wanted so badly not to remind people of
pennies, that I turned myself green." With
that Oliver was beginning to turn red.

Back at Battery Park suddenly it hit him. He could get a caricature of himself drawn!

"Excuse me sir." he exclaimed. "Would you draw me as a cartoon for this penny?" He could have guessed what was coming. The artist looked at the penny and got right to work, but when he turned his canvas around it simply read "No."

It was back to the drawing board for Oliver. As he walked across the park another unfamiliar voice reached out to him. It was his favorite! An NYPD Police dog.

24

"I knew a dog named Penny once." the dog explained. "He would sleep all day everyday. I bet if they named him Nickel or Quarter he wouldn't sleep all day. He would probably be a champion dog."

25

Oliver had always wanted
to hear a dog talk, but
so far he didn't like what
this one had to say.

On the walk home that evening Oliver was sad. He didn't want the mean pigeon or grumpy statue to be right, but he was beginning to think that they were.

*Maybe everyone is right, maybe you aren't worth
anything, maybe you aren't such good luck.* "No!"
Oliver interrupted his own thoughts. He didn't
come this far just to be wrong.

Oliver heard what sounded like a little girl crying from around the corner.

"Please sir, I can bring the rest back tomorrow? My puppy is hungry," said the girl who was about Oliver's age.

"Tough luck! Read the sign!" The old man shouted and pointed.

Dog Food

$1.01

Not $.99

Not $1.00

It's $1.01

Exactly!

32

The words "tough luck" made Oliver's heart beat a little faster. All she needed was a penny! Oliver extended his arm with the penny in hand.

"Excuse me sir, does this help?" The grumpy man accepted Oliver's lucky penny and handed the girl the dog food.

The girl immediately hugged Oliver, thanking him. She introduced herself, Lala. Oliver loved that name.

"I promise I will pay you back tomorrow!" Lala said to her new hero. "Don't worry about it," Oliver took a breath and observed the city. "It's just a penny," he said with a smile.

Oliver and Lala became inseparable. What started as another boring day became a true adventure. Talking pigeons, police dogs, and statues have all been proved wrong. Oliver got something with a penny that you couldn't get with one, one hundred, or one million dollars. A friend.

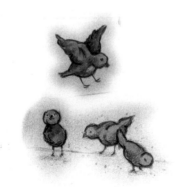

About The Artist

Lisa Lyman Adams is an award-winning illustrator, Fine Artist, and art instructor. Her signature style is a unique mix of super-realism, collage, and artists' handwriting. A regular contributor to mainstream magazines, *The New York Times*, and cover art for publishing houses, Lisa is also the author/illustrator of the popular holiday children's book, "The Twelve Days of Christmas in New York City."

Her art endures as the creator of the BabyGap Teddybear and her Strathmore Mixed Media paper pad covers. Represented by the Diane Birdsall Gallery in Old Lyme, CT, for her Fine Art, and affiliated with Morgan Gaynin, Inc. in New York City for her illustration, Lisa has been the recipient of numerous industry awards for both careers. She is a graduate of the Pratt Institute in Brooklyn, NY.